THE DAY
AFTER CHRISTMAS

by Alice Bach
pictures by Mary Chalmers

Harper & Row, Publishers

New York   Evanston   San Francisco   London

THE DAY AFTER CHRISTMAS
Text copyright © 1975 by Alice Hendricks Bach
Illustrations copyright © 1975 by Mary Chalmers

Library of Congress Catalog Card Number: 74–9073
Trade ISBN 0–06–020313–7
Harpercrest ISBN 0–06–020314–5

FIRST EDITION

For Anne Sexton, who is with me every day

Mother came into Emily's room and pulled up the shades. Pale winter sun shone on the quilt.

"Wake up," said Mother, wiggling Emily's foot. Emily scrunched up along the far side of the bed.

Yesterday before the sunlight fell on her quilt, Emily had tiptoed into the living room to look at all the packages spread out under the tree. Where was the candle she had made for Daddy? She had wrapped it in shiny gold paper. The other presents were covered with pictures of bells and holly and candy canes. She moved Daddy's present up front so he would see it right away. Then she crept back to her room and waited for Mother and Dad and Henry to wake up so Christmas could begin.

It's the day after Christmas, she thought. Everything is over.

"What do you want for breakfast, dear?" Mother asked.

"Steak and eggs." Emily sat up.

"Oh, Emily, that's a treat for Christmas morning. How about a soft-boiled egg with toast broken up in it?"

Emily threw herself against her pillow. "Yucck."

Mother sighed. "We can't have Christmas every day, dear." She left Emily alone.

Emily yanked on her bathrobe. She looked at Miss Mouse asleep on the fluffy white canopy bed in her new dollhouse. It was time for Miss Mouse to have her first breakfast in the dollhouse dining room. But Emily didn't care. She left Miss Mouse tucked under her organdy coverlet and went into the kitchen.

"Breakfast won't be ready for a few minutes, Emily. Why don't you get dressed?" Mother took orange juice, milk, and butter out of the refrigerator. All ordinary food.

Emily went into the living room and stood in front
of the tree. The ornaments were shiny red, blue, and
green. The point of the silver star touched the ceil-
ing, and the tinsel hung in shiny slices of light. The
sparkling tree reminded Emily of the round bits of
mirror on the Indian dress Grandmother had given
her for Christmas.

She ran back to her room and took the dress out
of the closet. The pieces of mirror shimmered in the
sunlight. They made Emily feel like Christmas again.

She put on the dress and smiled at herself in the
mirror. Then she tied a velvet ribbon in her hair
and skipped back into the kitchen.

Mother was pouring dry cereal into an everyday
bowl. Yesterday they had the dishes with Santa's face.

"That's a special dress for a special day," Mother
said. "Put on your regular slacks and a sweater."

Emily ran through the living room, ripping the ribbon from her hair. She threw the Indian dress on the floor.

Plain brown slacks, plain brown sweater. Ugly.

"I will not pour fresh water into the saucer under the tree," she said angrily. "I won't help Mother pack the ornaments into their boxes. Christmas is over and they can sweep it out of the house without me." She snatched the sprig of holly from her bulletin board and threw it into the wastebasket.

Emily sat at the kitchen table. She reached for
her cocoa. It had skin on it. She pushed it away.
  "Where's Daddy?"
  "At work."

16

At work, thought Emily, it's just a plain day. "Where's Henry?"

"Taking the clothes out of the dryer. Now hurry up and eat your cereal."

"I hate cereal." Emily scowled all the way back to her room.

"Want to play with my new milk truck, Em?"
"No."

Emily watched him pull his wooden truck along the rug. He was humming truck noises. The truck had a tiny row of milk bottles on the back. They rattled as Henry pulled the truck. Henry hummed louder. He pulled the truck up to Emily's dollhouse.

"Don't you wish Christmas was going to start this minute?"

"Want a milk delivery today, Lady?"

"Get out of my room, stupid," Emily shouted.

As Henry ran out, one of the bottles fell off his truck. Emily picked it up and tried to crush it in her hand.

Emily looked out the window. Everything was weighed down with snow. It stayed heavy on the trees and heavy on the ground. Nothing moved. The trees

were still. There were no cars and there were no people.
Emily wished the snow would melt. Right now.
A year is a very long time, Emily thought.

The doorbell rang. It was Robin, Emily's best friend.

"Hi, Em! What did you get? I got a chemistry set, some books, and my dad made me a wooden cradle like the pioneers had."

Emily didn't say anything.

Robin knelt beside the dollhouse. "Oh, Emily! Now Miss Mouse has her own house."

"So what," Emily said, turning away.

"Wallpaper! And a fireplace. The sink even has faucets!"

Emily wished it was the day before Christmas, the day before she had seen the dollhouse. There were no more surprises left. No packages were hidden in Mother's closet.

Robin walked her fingers up the dollhouse stairs.

"You're not sad at all." Emily stared at her friend. "Christmas is a whole year away."

Robin moved the doll's couch closer to the fireplace.

"Don't you care?" Emily screamed.

"I know Christmas is past," said Robin. "I had to feed the kittens before I was allowed to come over."

"But, Robin, we'll be halfway through third grade before it's Christmas again." Emily snatched up the couch.

She scratched a line in its velvet upholstery. The legs were carved wood, like Grandmother's couch.

It might be fun to make those stiff little pillows for the dollhouse couch. And something green for a rug in Miss Mouse's living room. Maybe Henry would give me the end off his bathrobe sash, thought Emily.

"I think it looks better against this wall," Emily
said, sliding the couch across the dollhouse floor.

Robin was busy shaping a chandelier out of bits
of tinfoil.

Emily flopped over on her stomach and ran her hand across the green shaggy rug. It was dry and didn't smell sweet like grass.

"In the spring, after the snow melts, we can take Miss Mouse's house outside. She will like the fresh breeze. We can put her couch on the grass and she can lie in the warm sun."

Emily whistled as she thought of Daddy's candle. He had unwrapped it carefully so he wouldn't tear the gold foil. Emily smiled for a long time. She could almost smell spring. She could almost see the tanned skin of summer.

Nothing was over except Christmas.

She walked over to the closet and picked up her Indian dress. She stroked it and hung it carefully in the closet. All by itself, away from her school clothes.

"Mom, can we have a tea party? With real milk and cookies?" Emily shouted.

"Take some of the gingerbread men hanging on the tree," Mother called.

"C'mon, Robin. You get Martha and Froggie off the bookshelf while I get Henry and the milk and cookies."

Robin looked at Emily. "How about Miss Mouse?"

Emily walked back to the dollhouse. She gently
lifted Miss Mouse from her canopy bed and cradled
her in her hand. She smoothed her white whiskers
and kissed the black tip of her pointy nose.

"Poor Miss Mouse. She's very hungry. She didn't
have any breakfast."

Christmas
Stories.

Christmas
Stories